WHEN THIS WORLD WAS NEW

by D.H. FIGUEREDO

illustrated by

ENRIQUE O. SANCHEZ

LEE & LOW BOOKS • *New York*

LEE & LOW BOOKS Inc., 95 Madison Avenue, New York, NY 10016

leeandlow.com

Manufacured in China by South China Printing Co.

Book Design by Christy Hale

Book Production by The Kids at Our House

The text is set in Weiss

The illustrations are rendered in acrylic on paper

(HC) 10 9 8 7 6 5 4 3 2

(PB) 10 9 8 7 6 5 4 3 2 1

First Edition

Library of Congress Cataloging-in-Publication Data

Figueredo, D.H.

When this world was new/by D.H. Figueredo; illustrated by Enrique O. Sanchez. —1st ed.

p. cm.

Summary: When his father leads him on a magical trip of discovery through new fallen snow,
a young boy who emigrated from his warm island home overcomes fears about living in New York.

ISBN 1-880000-86-5 (hardcover)   ISBN 1-58430-173-2 (paperback)

[1. Emigration and immigration—Fiction.   2. Fear—Fiction.   3. Snow—Fiction.

4. Fathers and sons—Fiction.]   I. Sanchez, Enrique O., 1942-ill.   II. Title.

PZ7.F488Wh 1999   [E]—dc21   98-53068   CIP AC

To my wife, Yvonne, my daughter, Gabriela—
and my son Daniel, who encouraged
me to write this story—D.H.F.

To Teresa Amelia—E.O.S.

It was our first day in this country. My parents and I came in the night before from an island on an ocean that was warm and far away.

We had to take two planes.

The first plane flew low over clear waters. I looked out the window at the boats beneath us. I saw large stingrays swimming near the surface of the sea. Papá looked out the window with me. He seemed worried. Mamá was very quiet.

We landed at a small airport near a beach. But we didn't stay there. We moved on to another plane. This was a jet. We flew high over the clouds and into the night.

I was excited. But I was also scared.

After a few hours in the air, we landed at a big airport. There were hundreds of people running from one end of the terminal to the other. They were carrying suitcases and packages and boxes. They didn't smile. They didn't speak in Spanish.

I took Mamá's hand and held it tightly.

At the gate, Uncle Berto was waiting. When he saw me, he called out my name, "Danilito, Danilito." He ran to greet us. He was happy. He was in this country alone. He was glad to have relatives around once again.

Uncle Berto led us to his car. He drove along a highway that was as long as a comet's tail. Cars sped past us as fast as meteors. The light shining through the windows of the tall buildings reminded me of the stars of a Caribbean night.

Uncle Berto was talking about America. He liked it here but said that winters were long and cold and that you could fall on ice and hurt yourself. He said that you had to speak English but it was not easy to learn a new language. And that "los americanos" were kind but there were a few who were not friendly toward foreigners.

I was a foreigner. And I didn't speak English. And I didn't know how to walk on ice.

I was scared.

Papá had worries, too. He wanted to take Mamá to a doctor. She had not been feeling well. She looked sad lately and she worried a lot.

He told Uncle Berto that in order to help Mamá, he needed money. To make money, he needed a job. But how could he find a job in a new country? How could he buy Mamá medicine? How could he buy food for us? And clothes? And rent an apartment?

Mamá nodded as Papá asked those questions. Uncle Berto nodded as well. He told Papá that everything would be fine, that it was just a matter of time.

Uncle Berto left the highway to cross a bridge. He drove down a ramp and up a hill and down a road that went through a park. Then, he slowed a bit and stopped in front of a house. It was a small house built of wood. It stood next to a clearing on the side of a small hill.

We went inside. There was a living room and a kitchen and two bedrooms. All the rooms had furniture.

Uncle Berto pointed at lots of cans of food on the kitchen table. "Comida para una semana," he said. Food for a week.

He pointed to a pile of winter clothes on a bed in one of the bedrooms. "Ropa de invierno," he said. Winter clothes.

He gave Papá the key.

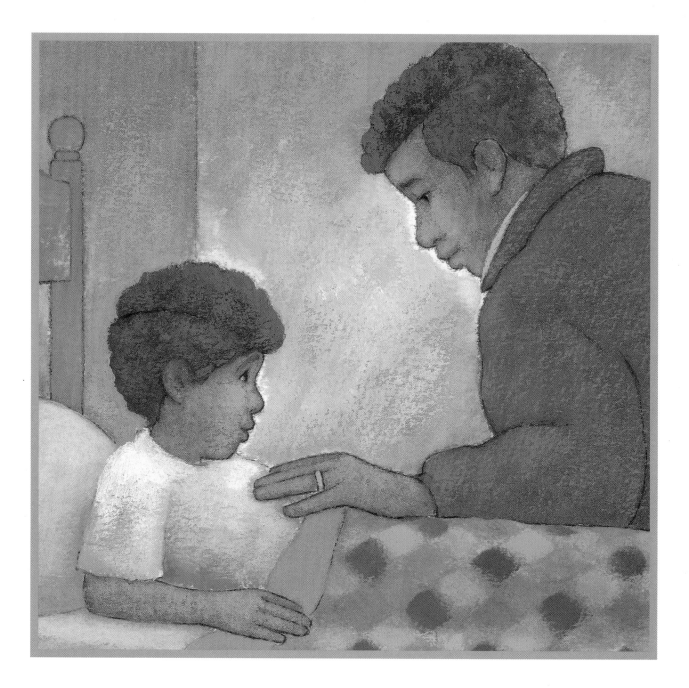

The next morning, Papá came into my bedroom. "Danilito," he
whispered. He wanted me to get up.

It was still dark. The shade on the window was down.

I sat on the edge of the bed. Papá had on clothes he'd never worn before:
boots, heavy pants, a coat, a scarf.

He helped me into a pair of boots. He gave me a coat. But my arms couldn't find the sleeves. I was not used to winter clothing.

I was still scared. Everything was happening so fast. On my first day here, I had to go to a new school where no one knew Spanish. How could I tell the teacher I had to go to the bathroom? How could I learn my lessons?

I told Papá that I should not go to school. I thought Uncle Berto should teach me some English first. But Papá said that I was a good student and that I would do well in any language. Then, he told me there was something he wanted me to see.

He took me to the living room. There, I saw a magic I had never seen before.

I ran to the window. Outside, there were millions of white rose petals floating downwards.

"Nieve," Papá said. Snow.

Buttoning his coat, he opened the door. I followed him out.

The front steps and the sidewalk and the street were all gone, vanished under a powder that was as white and fine as sugar. The parked cars had become polar bears. There were no sounds. All was still but for the falling snow.

Papá stepped on the sidewalk. I thought he might slip. But he
didn't. I stepped down. My feet sank softly into the snow.

I tilted my head backward. Flakes touched my face, melting on
my cheeks. Papá cupped his hands and shaped the snow into a ball.

He pitched it at a street sign. He missed, but didn't try again.
He wasn't wearing gloves and his hands were getting cold.

He turned to the field by the house. In the silence of the
snow, he trudged over.

The field rose gently. The snow falling on the clearing was so white
and pure it seemed as if a slice of a cloud had floated down to earth.
Papá began to walk towards the top of the hill. I walked beside him.

He was breathing hard, steam puffing from his mouth. His nose was red and shiny. His face was wet, as if bathed by a spray from a wave. It felt like we were walking on a sand dune but much colder.

The climb tired us. Our toes were icy and ticklish. Up to now, we had neither looked back nor down. We turned around and looked at the field. On the white, clear snow, we saw our footprints. The initial tracks were clumsy, crooked, leaning to one side. But the rest were deep and firm, one set of prints larger than the other.

Papá studied his footprints. "That's something I've always wanted to do," he said.

He placed his arm around me and we stood together, my body leaning against his. We didn't move, as if we were frozen. The gentle patches we had made stretched before us, a large signature on the expanse of a wide scroll.

The sound of a horn came from behind our house. It was Uncle
Berto in his car.

Neighbors began to come out. Shovels scraped the sidewalk.
Engines were turned on.

"We have to go," Uncle Berto called out.

Papá and I went back to the house to say good-bye to Mamá. She surprised us. She was not sleeping but was standing by the window. And she was smiling. It was the first time she had smiled in a long while.

She embraced Papá. Then, she kissed me.

Papá and I climbed into Uncle Berto's car. He said he'd take me to
school first and afterward he'd take Papá to a factory that needed workers.

As Uncle Berto drove past the field, I looked at our footprints in the
snow. Papá, sitting in the front, was also looking at the prints. He turned
to me. He smiled. I smiled back.

I was still scared.

But not as much.